The AMAZING DAYS of ABBY HAYES

Home Is Where the Heart Is

Read more books about me!

The AMAZING DAYS of ABBY HAYES

Home Is Where the Heart Is

ANNE MAZER

SCHOLASTIC INC.
New York Toronto London Auckland Sydney
Mexico City New Delhi Hong Kong Buenos Aires

ISBN 0-439-82924-0

12 11 10 9 8 7 6 5 4 3   8 9 10 11/0

Printed in the U.S.A.   40

First printing, June 2006

For Craig Walker

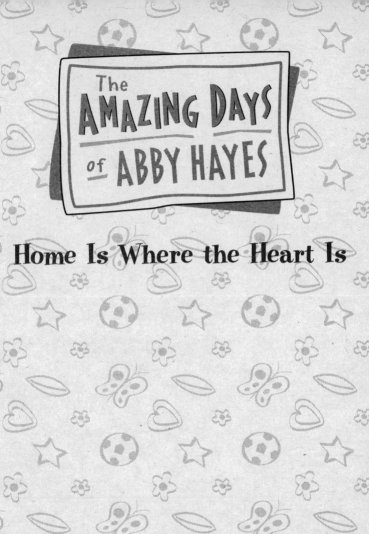

The AMAZING DAYS of ABBY HAYES

Home Is Where the Heart Is

Chapter 1

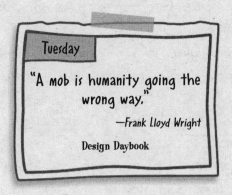

> **Tuesday**
>
> "A mob is humanity going the wrong way."
>
> —Frank Lloyd Wright
>
> **Design Daybook**

At seven o'clock this morning, there was a mob of humanity outside the bathroom door. We were ALL going the wrong way. . . .

<u>Inside the bathroom</u>:
My older sister Isabel, blow-drying her hair very, very, very slowly. She wouldn't come out.

<u>Outside the bathroom</u>:
My mother, my father, my little brother, Alex, and Isabel's twin, Eva. And me. We couldn't go in.

Eva had overslept and missed her shower time. She was late for a meeting with her basketball coach.

Alex had glue in his hair and needed to shampoo it out immediately, before it hardened.

It was officially my father's time to take a shower.

My mother had an emergency. She had to repair a fingernail before she left for work.

I just wanted to brush my teeth.

"I have a meeting to attend!" My mother banged on the bathroom door. "A VERY important meeting! The most important meeting of my life!! Isabel, do you hear me?"

My father was equally cranky. "Why isn't there any respect for rules in this family?" he grumbled. "We set up a perfectly good system for six people to use one bathroom and now no one follows it."

"My hair!" Alex shrieked. "It's turning hard! I'll have to shave my head! I'll be bald!"

"My coach won't put me in the next game if I'm late!" Eva cried.

I put my hand in front of my mouth
and checked for bad breath.

Suddenly, the door opened and Isabel
appeared.

Her long hair was glossy and curled.
She had showered, dressed, and put on
makeup.

"Good morning, dear family," Isabel said,
beaming at all of us. "Isn't it a beautiful
day?"

Wordlessly, my mother pushed past her.
The bathroom door slammed in our faces.

"No fair!" Eva cried.
My father muttered under his breath.
Alex started crying.
I scrubbed at my teeth with my forefinger.

Isabel stared at us as if we were all
crazy. "I don't know why the people in
this family are always in bad moods in the
morning."

I can tell her why.

<u>Three Reasons Why the People in</u>
<u>This Family Are Always in Bad</u>
<u>Moods in the Morning</u>

1. Certain teenage sisters hog the bathroom first thing every day.

2. One bathroom is shared by six people.

3. Everyone in the Hayes family is always in a rush, even on weekends. Except me. Lucky we live so close to everything.

I can't wait until it's time to go to school today.

"Your family seemed a little . . . um, frazzled this morning," Abby's best friend, Hannah, said as they walked to middle school with Mason, another close friend.

"That's putting it mildly," Abby said.

Just seeing her friends' cheerful faces was a relief. Abby could have hugged them when they showed up at her door.

"When we came to pick you up, it sounded like a madhouse," Mason said. "What was going on?"

"First, we had a major highway pileup in front

of the bathroom door," Abby explained. "Then, a few minutes later, Isabel and I collided in front of the dishwasher. Eva dropped a pitcher of juice in my father's lap. And my mother fell over Alex in the front hallway."

"Whew," Hannah said.

"We were like crazed bumper cars!" Abby said.

Mason teased, "Your family needs traffic arrows to point them in the right direction."

"Arrows? That's dangerous," Abby retorted. "I wouldn't put any kind of weapons in my sisters' hands."

"Nope," Hannah agreed. "I know Eva and Isabel. When they aren't getting along, stay out of the way. The sparks fly!"

"I've been burned many times," Abby said. She often wished that her sisters would stop fighting. But they almost never did. "At least I have my purple room to disappear into."

"You have one of the coolest rooms ever," Hannah said.

In fifth grade, Abby had painted her room a deep, rich purple. The desk, bookcase, chair, bedspread, and curtains were purple, too. It was like living inside a grape.

"It's my Purple Palace," Abby said. "Thank goodness I don't have to share it!"

Hannah sighed. "Not like me. My little sister Elena insists on sleeping in my room every single night. If I say no, she throws a terrible-twos tantrum."

Abby sighed in sympathy. She was lucky to have a room that was entirely hers. She was lucky to have a place where she felt so peaceful. And she was especially lucky to have friends who lived nearby and could rescue her when her family was just too much to take.

As the three friends crossed the street, they saw streams of kids heading toward the school. Yellow buses were turning into the drive.

"There's Simon!" Hannah exclaimed.

Abby's heart pounded. Her face suddenly felt hot. She had a crush on Simon. Only Hannah knew about it.

"And Natalie's with him," Hannah said.

"Natalie?" Abby repeated in surprise. "I didn't know they were friends again."

Hannah shrugged. "Why shouldn't Natalie and Simon be friends? They're musicians, aren't they? They're part of the same band."

Abby didn't reply. She knew a secret about Natalie that only she and Simon shared. Natalie seemed uncomfortable around her and Simon now, even though Abby had kept her promise to not tell anyone. She hadn't even told Hannah. Simon had kept Natalie's secret, too, as far as she knew.

"What's the big deal about Simon?" Mason suddenly demanded. "All the girls in this school are googly-eyed about him."

"Not *all*," Hannah said. "Not me!"

"Not me, either," Abby quickly said. It wasn't really a lie. She had a crush on him, but she wasn't googly-eyed about Simon. At least, she hoped not.

"So what is it about him?" Mason said again.

"He's smart, talented, and really nice." Abby blushed. "And he's cute," she added.

Mason didn't look pleased.

Hannah poked him. "You're cute, too, Mason," she said playfully.

"Nah," Mason said. "Not me."

"You've changed since elementary school," Abby said.

It was true. Since fifth grade, Mason had slimmed down and shot up. If he wasn't such an old friend and if she wasn't so used to thinking of him as the

Chapter 2

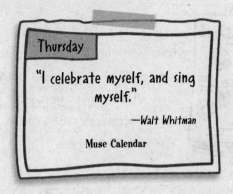

Thursday

"I celebrate myself, and sing myself."

—Walt Whitman

Muse Calendar

Did Walt Whitman know Brianna?

Brianna is one of the most popular girls in sixth grade. She wears the best clothes, gets the best grades, is the best actor in the school, has the most famous relatives, and is the only person in our town who's been featured in television commercials.

Remember: Brianna starts with the letter B. And B means BEST.

It also means BOAST. Wherever you see Brianna, you'll hear her bragging. She loves to celebrate herself. Every day is Brianna Day.

Today Ms. Bean, our art teacher, gave us a new assignment. We are going to cut out magazine images, photos, and pictures to create collages about ourselves.

Now Brianna is planning a major Brag-Fest. She has already started to brag about the glossy model shots, playbills from theater productions, and rave reviews she's going to include. She'll also have photos of herself on horseback, and in a ballet tutu, as well as pictures of her perfect family on their yacht.

Is there such a thing as "brag sickness"? I think I might be coming down with it.

What Other Kids Are Making

Victoria, the meanest girl in sixth grade, is planning a fashion collage. She is going to photograph her entire wardrobe and paste it on posterboard.

Will she make herself into a paper doll?

If I said that to Victoria, I'd end up with a paper cut, or two or three.

Mason is making a collage of monkeys, apes, and baboons. He says they remind him of his family. (Ha-ha. This is just like Mason. And I bet his mother, Betsy, will laugh, too, when he tells her.)

Sophia, my new middle-school friend, will do a collage of her drawings. I bet it'll be beautiful! She is a really good artist.

Hannah is gathering her favorite images: rainbows, tropical fish, waterfalls, and birds. Even though the collage won't have a single picture of Hannah, it will still be totally HER.

What should <u>I</u> do?

Hannah suggested an all-purple collage.

<u>Why I can't</u>
If I hang it up in my room afterward, I won't be able to see it. It'll blend in with my purple walls.

Sophia suggested that I tear out my journal pages and make a writing assemblage.

Why I can't
I would NEVER put my journal writings on the wall for everyone to read.

Mason told me to make a chocolate-chip-cookie collage.

Why I can't
Ever since Mason and I got detention for selling cookies in the school yard, I get ill at the thought of chocolate-chip cookies.

So what should I do?

Ms. Bean suggested a collage of family photos. YES!!!!
I'll find scenes from Hayes family life and paste them together. Ms. Bean said the collage could highlight our good times and humorous moments.
Too bad I didn't take any photos this morning when everyone was fighting over the bathroom.

That wasn't a good time, but it wasn't a bad time, either. Now that it's over, it was actually kind of funny.

Abby sat on the living room floor with an open photo album in front of her. Frowning, she thumbed through the pages.

There was a photograph of her sister Eva winning a race at the age of ten; and Eva's twin, Isabel, as class president at twelve. Her younger brother, Alex, stood in front of his prize-winning science-fair exhibit when he was in first grade.

Abby turned the pages. There was Eva again, the junior high school captain of every girls' sports team. She ran across finish lines, batted home runs, and swished balls into baskets.

After that, a section of the album was devoted to Isabel. There was a photo of her in the state capitol, winning a debate competition, and then another one of her in the lead role in a middle school play. Abby turned a page to find Alex posing with a robot he had designed and made.

It was depressing to see how brilliant her siblings were. Did they ever do anything that was less than outstanding? Did her parents ever take a picture of it?

Where were the pictures of Isabel admiring her fingernails, or Alex with glue in his hair? Where was Eva spilling orange juice all over her father?

And what about Abby? Where was *she*?

The pictures she found were ordinary. She was selling old toys at a garage sale or combing her curly red hair while sticking out her tongue at the camera. There she was again, covered with flour, baking the chocolate-chip cookies that got her into so much trouble with the principal.

"Exciting," she muttered sarcastically.

Abby liked to tell herself that her honors were forgotten since she was the middle child. But she sometimes worried it was because her accomplishments were so much less, well . . . *accomplished* than her siblings'.

Or maybe it was because Abby excelled at things that were quiet and private. Like writing. How did you take pictures of *that*?

But she had gotten off track. She was searching for the good times and humorous moments of the Hayes family. Where were the photos of siblings hugging, or clowning around in the living room, or jumping into ponds in the summer?

Was the Hayes family too busy overachieving

to have warm, cozy, cuddly moments? Unless you counted the time that the furnace broke down and the entire family had huddled under her parents' down comforter in the living room. *That* was family togetherness.

But no one had taken pictures. It had been too cold.

Abby placed the photo album back on the coffee table, stood up, and brushed off her pants.

Forget about the family collage.

But now what?

A purple collage, like Hannah suggested?

Abby sighed. She guessed it didn't matter if it blended into her wall. It was the next best idea. She'd collect a bunch of old magazines and cut out pictures of purple flowers, clothes, signs, and mountains.

There was only one small problem: As she looked around the house, she couldn't find any magazines. They had disappeared from the house.

Abby went into the kitchen. Her parents were talking in low voices. They stopped as soon as she came in.

"Mom? Dad?" she asked. "What happened to the magazines?"

"They were lying around for months. So I recycled

them," her mother said.

"Are they still in the bin?"

Her mother shook her head. "They got picked up with the garbage this morning."

Abby groaned. "I need them for a school assignment!"

"Sorry, honey. If you had let me know earlier, I would have saved them. Next time, give me some advance notice."

"Why do I have to give notice to save old magazines?" Abby cried. "If we were like everyone else, we'd have ten years' worth of old, useless magazines just begging to be cut up for a collage."

"I don't think we're like everyone else," her father said mildly.

"We're not." Abby sighed. In an ordinary family, she might have been smart and talented. In this family, she didn't have a chance. "But *now* what am I supposed to do for my collage?"

"Use your calendars?" her father suggested.

"My calendars!" She had been collecting calendars forever. She owned hundreds of them—and every single one was precious to her. "I can't believe you'd even say that."

"You have stacks of them in your room," her father said. "There must be one or two that you could take apart."

"Good idea," her mother agreed. "Get rid of some of that clutter."

"My calendars are not clutter!" Abby said indignantly. "They're *friends*."

Her father shrugged. "It's entirely up to you. But if you need pictures for your art class assignment . . ." He left the sentence unfinished.

"No!" Abby cried angrily. *"Never!"* She rushed from the room. The last thing she'd ever do was cut up one of her calendars. Why couldn't anyone in her family understand that? Why couldn't anyone in her family understand *her*?

Chapter 3

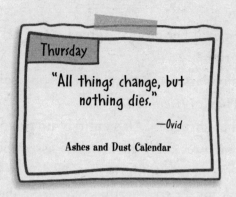

Thursday

"All things change, but
nothing dies."

—Ovid

Ashes and Dust Calendar

Is that true?

If I changed a few, <u>just a few</u>, of my
calendars into a collage, would I be giving
them a new life?

Or would they die?

Calendar Count

Frog, Mouse, Horse, Pig, Butterfly, and
other animal calendars: 57

Mountain, Ocean, Sky, Ice, Flower, and
other nature calendars: 93

Wizards, Mothers, Police, Teachers, and
other people calendars: 81

Funny, Silly, Humorous, and Ridiculous calendars: 34

State Capital, Farm, Coffee Shop, and other place calendars: 75

Art, History, Music, Poetry, and Travel calendars: 96

Weird calendars: 42

Total Number of Calendars in Abby Hayes's Room: approximately 478

<u>Calendar Locator (or Where to Find the Approximately 478 Calendars in My Room)</u>

On walls

In desk drawers

Under bed

At back of closet shelf

On floor

Below pillow

I took out all of my calendars. I looked at each and every one to decide which one I MIGHT use for a collage.

Calendar Cut Count

Calendars that must NEVER be cut up: 433

Calendars that I prefer NOT to cut up: 37

Calendars that I MIGHT cut up, but only if I have to: 4

Calendars that I don't mind cutting up, at least not TOO much: 2

Calendars that are PROBABLY okay to cut up, although I'd really rather not: 1

On the Other Hand . . .

Unless my house turns into a calendar museum, only a few calendars can hang on my walls at a time.

Most of my calendars are in corners or closets.

No one ever sees them.

They are condemned to a sad life of darkness and loneliness.

One day, my mother will enter the room in one of her "clean and destroy" moods,

and that will be the end of my beloved
calendars.

Poor calendars!!!!!

I am practically crying now. Do my calendars <u>want</u> me to cut them up? Are they
telling me to take their most colorful images
to make a collage that the world will see
and admire?

My mother would never throw out a collage.

I am going to pick up my scissors and
boldly make the first cut. . . .

<u>A few hours later</u>: That
was more fun than I imagined.

My floor is filled with hundreds of
cut-out calendar images: clowns, pigs,
toothbrushes, mustaches, striped socks, opera
singers, outhouses, sailboats, raindrops . . .

And my collage is filled with strange,
beautiful, and funny things.

* * *

I love my collage. I can't wait to see what Ms. Bean says when she sees it.

When I finished the assignment, I didn't want to stop. So I turned my journal cover into a famous-writer collage. On the inside of my journal, I pasted pictures of pens, computers, and typewriters.

My calendars have found a new life! I think I've found a new hobby!

Chapter 4

Friday

"All is change."

—Euripides

Cycling Calendar

Even though I don't have art class
until next Tuesday, I brought my collage
to school to show to Ms. Bean. She liked
it! She hung it on the wall for all her art
classes to see.

Hooray!!!

Ms. Bean asked what inspired my collage.
I said, "Calendars."

It's funny to think it began with a pile
of calendars.

The calendars changed into images on my floor.

The images changed into a collage. (And a big mess that I still haven't cleaned up.)

The collage changed into an exhibit in Ms. Bean's art room.

Maybe I'll write about the collage for the literary journal and change it into a bunch of words!!!

The front door slammed behind Abby. "I'm home!" she yelled, putting down her backpack.

Her father appeared. He was carrying a box of books. His face was smudged with dirt. "Hi, Abby. Will you open the front door for me?"

Abby swung the door open again. "Recycling?"

"Cleaning out the attic," her father replied. "Getting rid of belongings we don't need or use."

"Don't go in *my* room," Abby said. "I don't want a single thing thrown out. Especially the stuff on the floor."

"You might want to pick up before your mother sees the mess," Paul Hayes advised. He stepped onto the porch. "You know how she gets. By the way, we're going out to dinner tonight. Our favorite Mexican restaurant."

Abby frowned. "I thought it was Isabel's turn to make dinner."

"You prefer your sister's cooking to Mexican food?"

"No," Abby admitted. "But it's not fair that she gets out of cooking."

"Someday you'll get a break, too." Her father set the books down on the stairs. "Your mother and I have something exciting to tell you tonight."

"What?"

"You'll have to wait and see," her father said with a smile. "But I think you'll like it."

The Hayes family sat around a big table in the corner of the Mexican restaurant. There was only one empty chair. Their mother hadn't arrived yet. She had called to say that she was going to be a few minutes late.

Paul Hayes sipped at a root beer. Alex fidgeted with his napkin. Isabel and Eva whispered to each other.

Abby leaned closer to catch what they were saying. But they didn't want her to hear.

"Quit eavesdropping," Isabel said to her.

"We weren't talking to *you*," Eva added rudely.

"It's not polite to whisper at the dinner table," Abby said. "Isn't that right, Dad?"

"Abby. Isabel. Eva." Their father pronounced their names slowly and patiently. "Tonight is a special evening. I don't know why you're arguing, but can you please stop *now*?"

"It's *their* fault," Abby said.

"It's always our fault," Eva said.

Isabel leaned toward their father. "Dad, why is tonight so special? Can't you tell us? Or at least give us a hint?"

Their father cleared his throat. "I promised your mother I wouldn't break the news before she arrived. It's her news, anyway. You wouldn't want me to break a promise, would you?"

"*Yes,*" Abby, Alex, Eva, and Isabel chanted in a rare moment of agreement.

He picked up his menu. "Change of subject," he announced. "What do you want to eat tonight?"

"I want a cheeseburger," Alex said. He was always hungry.

"This is a Mexican restaurant," their father explained. "They don't have cheeseburgers."

"Besides, cheeseburgers clog up your arteries with all that fat," Eva added.

Isabel made a face. "Do you mind not giving us the disgusting details?"

"He needs to be educated," Eva insisted.

Alex shook his head. "I want a cheeseburger and fries," he said again.

"You can have enchiladas," Paul said. "Or nachos or a quesadilla."

"I'm having something healthy," Eva announced. "Rice and beans."

"Ugh," Isabel said. "Boring."

Their father sighed and shook his head. "Your mother will be here any minute. Can we have a five-minute truce, please?"

Abby looked up. "There she is now. Mom!"

Olivia Hayes slid into a seat next to her husband. She was wearing a pale blue silk suit and a matching floral scarf. She looked the same as always, but somehow different.

Abby stared at her, trying to figure out what the difference was. Her mother seemed to glow. She looked radiant and happy. Whatever news she had, it had to be good.

"Mom, can I have a cheeseburger?" Alex said.

"Honey, it's a Mexican restaurant. You like the chicken burritos, remember?"

"Oh, yeah," Alex said.

"What's up, Mom?" Isabel said eagerly. "We're dying to know."

Olivia smiled. "Wait. I'll tell you after we order our food."

Eva leaned over to whisper to Isabel. "She's in a *very* positive mood."

"I heard that," Abby said to her sisters.

"So?" Isabel said.

The waiter appeared at the side of the table. "Ready?" he asked, taking out his pad.

"What is everyone having?" Paul asked.

"Rice and red beans, of course," Eva said with a superior air.

"I'll have the super nacho plate," Isabel said, with an equally superior air. "With extra sour cream and guacamole."

"Me, too," Olivia said, "but without the sour cream."

"I'll have, um, a plate of nachos," Abby said. "Just regular."

"A chicken burrito for Alex and a beef taco for me," Paul said.

The waiter scrawled their orders on his pad and disappeared into the kitchen.

There was a moment of silence.

Then Paul took Olivia's hand. "We—I mean, your mother has some wonderful news to announce."

"A new Hayes family member?" Eva blurted out. Then she turned bright red.

Isabel's eyes widened.

"Hooray!" Alex cried. "I'm sick of being the youngest!"

"A little sister?" Abby said hopefully. She loved the way Hannah's sister, Elena, followed her around, imitating everything she said and did.

"If we're having a baby, *I'm* the babysitter," Isabel announced.

Paul held up his hand. "Whoa! Wait a minute!"

"We're not having another child," Olivia said. "The four of you are more than enough."

Alex looked disappointed. "We're not?"

"Tell them the good news," Paul urged.

"I got a promotion," their mother announced.

"That's it?" Eva said.

"Congratulations, Mom," Isabel said politely. "I'm sure you deserve it."

"Yeah," Alex mumbled.

"Great, Mom," Abby said. Why did adults get excited over such silly things? The promotion was probably just another title or a bunch of initials after her mother's name. Didn't her mother have enough of those already?

A new baby would have been so much better.

"It's not an ordinary promotion," her mother was saying. "The firm is opening a new law office in another town. Guess who's in charge?"

"You?" Alex said.

Their mother nodded proudly. "It'll practically be like having my own firm," she said. "Except it's better, because I'll still have my partners. And I'm getting a *gigantic* raise."

"Why didn't you say so in the first place?" Eva cried.

"Hooray, Mom!" Abby cheered. More money, a new office—that was something that the entire family could applaud.

Alex said, "Are we rich now?"

"Even a little bit richer?" Abby echoed. Just a few months ago, she'd had to earn money for summer writing camp by baking thousands of cookies. It had been a high price to pay.

If her parents had extra money now, maybe they'd

invest in a few things for her. Like a television for her room. Or a portable music player. Or her own laptop computer.

"Wait a minute, hold on," Paul said, picking up his spoon and tapping it on his water glass for attention. "You haven't heard everything yet. We have another surprise in store for you."

Just as Olivia began to speak, the waiter arrived with their hot food.

"Thank you, this looks fabulous," Paul said. He picked up his fork and knife.

"I'm starved," Olivia said, unfolding her napkin. "I haven't eaten all day."

But no one else even looked at their food.

"Don't torture us any longer, Mom," Isabel begged. "Tell us, what's the surprise? A new car?"

"A supercomputer?" Alex said.

"A fantastic family vacation?" Abby said.

"Tickets to the Olympics?" Eva said.

Olivia finished chewing before she answered. "Better than all of those. We're buying a new house closer to my new job. We're moving, everyone!"

There was a moment of shocked silence. Then, as if on cue, Eva and Isabel burst into tears.

Chapter 5

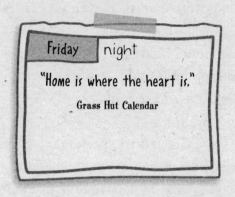

Friday night

"Home is where the heart is."

Grass Hut Calendar

Home is where a lot of hearts are. Like Isabel's, Eva's, Alex's, and mine.

For once, the Hayes siblings are in complete and total agreement. None of us want to move.

Our parents have assured us that we won't have to change schools. Our school district includes many areas on the outskirts of town. But we are all against buying a new house.

Isabel and Eva's Reasons for Never Leaving Our House

This is the house where they had birthday parties, water-balloon fights, cookouts, and sleepovers. This is the house where they memorized speeches, rehearsed for plays, and practiced their basketball dunks. This is the house that they both love.

Alex's Reasons

He was born here. He started school here. His robots live here. His computer is happy here. He's happy here.

My Reasons

I don't want to be far away from my friends!

I want to keep walking to and from school every day with Mason and Hannah.

I never want to leave my purple room!

We all tried to make our parents change their minds. But even though we outnumbered them four to two, we didn't convince them.

They've already made their decision . . . without us.

Isabel spoke for all of us. "What happened to the Hayes family democracy?" she asked. "Don't we have a voice? Don't you care about how WE feel?"

Our father said, "This is a very important time for your mother and we have to support her."

Then he listed their reasons.

<u>Our Parents' Reasons for Moving</u>
1. Only one bathroom in our house. (Okay, he has a point there.)
2. Our dining room isn't formal enough to entertain my mom's new clients and partners.
3. She needs to live closer to her new office, which is more than an hour away from our present home.
4. Dad can work anywhere.
5. We can now afford a bigger, nicer house.

Okay, I understand their reasons. But why do my parents have to pick up and leave everything we love? Couldn't they at least TRY to find a way to stay?

Isabel, Eva, Alex, and I want to support our mother. But not if it means getting rid of our beloved home!

"Pick up, Hannah!" Abby ordered. She held the telephone to her ear, praying that her best friend was home.

The Hayes family had just returned from the restaurant. Alex had retired to his room in tears. Isabel and Eva had stormed out of the house. Abby had grabbed the phone and taken it to her room.

Hannah's phone rang again and again. Abby jabbed the OFF button, then pushed the ON button to dial Mason's number.

"Hello. Good evening," Mason's mother, Betsy, answered the phone. "Whom do you wish to speak to?"

"Hello?" Abby cried. "It's Abby! Is Mason there?"

Betsy seemed delighted to hear from her. "How *are* you, Abby?"

"I need to speak to Mason right away. Please," she added, in case that was rude.

Without another word, Betsy handed the phone to Mason.

"Yo, what's up?" he said.

"Mason, I . . ." Abby stammered. "I . . . We . . . My . . ."

"Abby?"

"My family, we . . ."

"Are you okay?"

"No, I'm not," Abby managed to say. "We . . . I . . ." She couldn't get any further. "Can you come over?" she finally said.

Abby called Casey, Bethany, and Natalie. She wasn't as close to Bethany and Natalie as she used to be, but it didn't matter now. She wanted them to know what was happening.

She called Hannah over and over until she reached her. She called Sophia, who wasn't home. Now almost all of her friends, past and present, were crowding into her room. Besides Sophia, only her former best friend, Jessica, who had moved to Oregon last year to live with her father and his new family, was missing.

Abby scooped up the cutout images that littered the floor to clear a space for her friends. She hoped her eyes weren't swollen from crying.

"This is an emergency all-friends meeting," Abby announced. She twisted a tissue in her hand. "I have something sad to tell you."

Her friends looked concerned.

Hannah hugged her. "We love you, Abby."

Bethany said, "Don't worry, we're here."

"We'll fix it," Mason insisted. "Whatever it is."

Abby took a deep breath. "My mother got this big promotion and" — her voice trembled a little — "she's got to commute really far, so we're . . ." She couldn't get the words out.

It was Natalie who said them for her. "You're not moving away!" she cried. "No, not you!"

Abby nodded mutely.

"You *can't* leave!" Casey said.

Mason looked very upset. "What will we do without you?"

"I'll be in school," Abby said slowly. "My parents promised to stay in the same district." She hoped they would keep their promise.

"That's not so bad," Bethany said. "At least you're not leaving, like Jessica. At least we'll be able to see you."

"But it *won't* be the same!" Abby cried. "I'll be out of the neighborhood. I won't be able to meet you at the pool every afternoon during the summer, or ride my bike with you in the park whenever I want, or call you up and ask you to come over for an emergency all-friends meeting."

"When is this happening?" Hannah said in dismay.

"Soon," Abby said.

"That *stinks*," Mason said. "Why don't you come live at my house? We have an extra room." He turned bright red as he said it.

"Or mine," Hannah said. "If you can stand my sister pulling all your clothes out of drawers and trying to put them on."

"You can stay over at my house anytime," Bethany chimed in. "Especially if you like hamsters."

"I'd invite you to mine if I didn't hate it so much," Natalie said in a low voice.

Abby blinked back tears. "You guys are the greatest."

"Remember, we're always your friends," Mason said. "Even if you live far away."

"I wish I *could* stay with all of you," Abby said. Maybe her parents would let her rotate visits? She tried to imagine herself staying a week at Hannah's house, then another week at Bethany's.

She'd be like the kid of divorced parents, except it would be a house divorce.

"Ask them," Casey urged.

Abby sighed. "It's a terrific idea, but they'd never agree to it."

"How are you getting to school? Is your father going to drive you? Will you take a school bus?" Hannah asked.

"I don't know," Abby said.

"Where exactly is your new house?" Natalie asked.

"I don't know," Abby said again. "I don't think my parents have found one yet." She wondered if her parents would consult her and her siblings about the house. She hoped so. But suddenly she didn't trust that they would. They'd sprung the move on them out of nowhere.

There were so *many* things she didn't know. Like what her new house would look like and where it would be. Whether she'd still have her own room. If she'd be allowed to paint it purple again. How she would get to school. How she would ever manage to see her friends. Whether they would slowly forget her when she was out of sight . . . and whether she'd be too far away to do anything about it.

Chapter 6

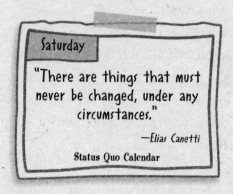

Saturday

"There are things that must never be changed, under any circumstances."

—Elias Canetti

Status Quo Calendar

Right.

I am taking this quote, printing it in huge black letters, and placing it on my parents' plates before breakfast this morning.

Will they get the message?

My friends tried to cheer me up last night. But after they left, I felt sadder than ever.

Now if I need my friends, they're here right away.

Now if Hannah wants me to help watch her little sister, Elena, she can call me on the spur of the moment.

Now if Mason wants to invite me to a basketball game, his mother can swing by the house and pick me up.

Now if Bethany's hamsters have babies, I can stop by her house on the way home to see them.

Now if Casey wants to come over and play basketball in our yard, he can just ring the doorbell.

When we move, it'll be so much more difficult to see each other. I'll be all alone in a strange neighborhood.

No emergency all-friends meetings. No last-minute sleepovers in tents in my backyard. No front- or back-porch evening parties.

Why are my parents taking us away from all this? I don't think they understand what we're losing.

At Saturday morning breakfast with her family, Abby stared at the crack in the kitchen ceiling, trying to memorize its shape. When she was younger, she used to imagine it was a face watching her.

This is one of the last times I will ever see that face in the ceiling, she told herself.

"Will the new house have cracks in the ceiling?" she asked her mother.

"Of course not!" Olivia Hayes replied. "We're going to have a brand-new, gorgeous house."

"This one is good enough for me," Abby said.

"But wait until you see our new kitchen," her mother said. She was extremely cheerful this morning again.

"Cherry cupboards, ceramic floor, stainless-steel appliances, a professional cook's stove . . ." their father recited.

Isabel looked upset. "It sounds like you've picked the house out already," she said.

Their mother shook her head. "Not yet. We circled some properties in the real estate section of the paper today. But we haven't looked at them yet."

Isabel let out a long sigh of relief. "You *are* going to consult us before you buy anything, aren't you?"

"We demand to be included," Eva said.

"Yes," Abby said.

Their parents didn't reply.

"Exactly what kind of house are *we* looking for?" Isabel asked, folding her arms across her chest.

"One with cathedral ceilings, a working fireplace, larger bedrooms, and an office space for me," Paul said.

"And a four-car garage for when Eva and Isabel start driving," Olivia added. "You see, girls, we *are* thinking of you."

"Don't think about us," Isabel said. "*Ask* us. We want to be part of the decision making. I'd rather have that than garage space."

"Hear, hear!" Eva cried.

Abby and Alex clapped their hands in support of the twins.

As the four siblings cheered one another on, Abby realized that something unusual was happening. The Hayes siblings were united. They were supporting one another. They were acting like a team. If there was one good thing about this move, it was their new togetherness. But did it have to take *this* to bring them together?

"All of you kids will have bigger rooms and a bathroom for yourselves," their father continued.

Olivia added, "We want to find a house with a library, too. Abby and Isabel, you'll love it."

A picture of a quiet, book-lined room with reading lamps, small couches, and maybe even a window seat flashed through Abby's mind. But then Isabel interrupted the tempting thought.

"I know what I love," Isabel said. "*This* house has everything I need. I don't think we should move at all."

"Me, neither." Abby hurried to second her older sister. With Isabel on her side, they just *might* win this one. "I *love* my room and everything here."

Olivia smiled. "When you see the new house, you won't ever look back," she promised.

"That's not true!" Alex said.

"I'll never forget this house!" Abby cried. How could she forget the friendly creak of the attic stairs? Or the lilac tree in the backyard? Or the light that came through the hallway window in the morning?

Not to speak of all the sad and happy moments, the fights and the family celebrations that had happened here.

"Sorry, kids. Our minds are made up," Paul said. "The decision is final. It's just one of those things. You'll have to get used to it. And honestly, when we find the right house, we'll have to act quickly. I want to make your mother's transition to her new job as smooth as possible."

"Is this *you* speaking, Dad?" Abby said. Her father always listened to what she and her siblings had to say.

Paul shrugged. "Your mother's work comes first," he said. "This isn't like picking a vacation spot."

Isabel's eyes flashed. She looked like she was about to unfold a very persuasive and scathing argument, but she was interrupted by the phone.

Olivia jumped up to answer it. "Home of the Hayeses," she said.

"Not for much longer," Eva muttered.

"Marissa! I was waiting for your call. Yes, we're selling our house. We'd like to list it with you . . ." Olivia disappeared into another room. The sound of her voice slowly faded as she shut a door behind her.

"Is that a real estate agent?" Isabel asked in horror.

Their father nodded.

Abby stared at the second hand on the clock. How much time did she have left in her beloved house and neighborhood?

Olivia came back into the kitchen. "Great news!

The real estate agent will be here later today to take photos," she said. "We're putting the house on the market on Monday."

"On *Monday*?" Eva cried. "That's only two days from now!"

"Can't you wait a few weeks?" Abby begged.

"But my basketball championship games!" Eva said.

"No!" Alex said. "NO!"

"This is the selling season. Property is going fast in this neighborhood," their father said. "Some lucky family is going to snap up our house really fast."

Lucky? That word definitely didn't apply to Abby or her siblings. Soon some other kid would be living in her purple room. Soon another family would take over their house.

"What if no one wants our house?" Eva said hopefully. "Will we cancel the move?"

"No, Eva," their mother said. "We're going to sell the house."

The words had a final ring to them. Abby, Isabel, Eva, and Alex looked at one another in dismay.

"Today we'll get the house ready for viewing," their father said. "Everyone needs to chip in. Get into your cleaning clothes and meet us downstairs. Your mother and I will hand out work assignments."

"Assignments? Is this school?" Eva grumbled.

Isabel said something under her breath about forced labor.

"We should go on strike," Abby said without much conviction. Any rebellion was bound to be crushed. What could she and her siblings do? They were kids, not adults. It seemed like the adults were making all the decisions. What Abby and her siblings wanted or needed didn't matter.

At least, that's the way it was in this new Hayes family.

Chapter 7

Thursday

"He is happiest who finds peace in his home."

—Goethe

Fireside Calendar

There's no peace in <u>this</u> home.

<u>Unpeaceful Happenings in the Unhappy Home of the Hayes</u>

1. <u>The Room Cleaning</u>
Of course, we had to clean our rooms. It wasn't the usual cleaning, either. Not only did we have to vacuum, dust, and make our beds, but we had to get rid of all the clutter.

<u>What My Mother USED to Call Clutter</u>:

1. crumpled papers and wrappers that accidentally missed wastebasket
2. dirty clothes tossed on floor for week or more
3. empty soda cans, water bottles, and stale pretzels or popcorn

If my mother hadn't made me clean up that clutter, my room would have turned into a giant purple trash can. Okay. She was right about that.

But now that we're putting our house on the market, clutter isn't what it used to be.

<u>What My Mother NOW Calls Clutter</u>:

1. calendars
2. books and papers
3. collage materials
4. earrings, hairbrush, and barrettes
5. stuffed animals and sports equipment
6. backpack
7. me???

My so-called clutter was minding its own private business in its own carefully selected places.

(Okay, maybe they weren't so carefully selected. Maybe they were just places where I found a free spot to drop something. But so what?)

My so-called clutter wasn't bothering anyone.

It wasn't growing germs or hideous green mold.

It wasn't tripping people up when they came into my room.

My clutter wasn't making decisions that everyone hated. (Like certain other people I won't mention.)

But my mother wouldn't listen to a single argument.

She just said, "Abby, everything has to be put away by noon today. Or I'll come in here with a garbage bag and do it myself."

When my mother says that, I know she's serious.

So I cleaned up the clutter.

(Note: What she called clutter was really my STUFF. And my STUFF doesn't like being called clutter. In fact, my STUFF had its feelings hurt. It wants to ask my mother for an apology, but she is too busy smiling all the time and describing how wonderful our new house will be. These days it doesn't matter <u>whose</u> feelings she hurts.)

2. <u>The House Cleaning</u>

The room cleaning was bad. The house cleaning was even worse.

We put away every envelope, dish, and pair of scissors. We straightened every pillow on the couch and fixed all the crooked pictures on the wall. We washed every window, we polished every wooden surface.

When we finished, Eva said, "It doesn't look like anyone lives here." She didn't mean it as a compliment.

My parents looked pleased, though. They ignored our grumbling and said, "Great job, kids. Now we're ready for the real estate agent."

3. The Real Estate Agent

Marissa is very tall and very thin. She was wearing a red jacket and white pants and lots of gold jewelry. She was friendly and talked to the kids as well as the parents. I would have liked her if she was someone else's real estate agent.

She took pictures of the house, both inside and out. She also measured the rooms, looked inside closets, checked out the basement and attic, and asked lots and lots of boring questions about the roof, furnace, flooding in the basement, insulation, and electrical wiring.

And then she made suggestions. She said to put flowers on the porch to make the house look welcoming.

She said we needed to do more straightening up. We have to take all appliances off the counters and clean out the closets. Everything is going into the attic until the house sells.

"The emptier, the better," she said. "That way people can imagine themselves living here."

She also told my parents to do some

"cosmetic repairs" to make the house look more attractive.

My father called a handyman who is coming in tomorrow to repair and repaint.

After Marissa left, my parents took me aside. They said that Marissa had advised them to repaint my room. She thinks a shiny purple room will scare buyers away. They are going to repaint my perfect Purple Palace!

I asked my parents if they decided someday that they didn't want a curly, redheaded daughter, would they exchange me for a model with straight black hair? They said not to be silly.

I said I loved my room as much as they loved me.

They said a room is not a person.

But a room can be as important as a person!!!

My siblings agreed. They tried to convince our parents to leave my room alone. They said that one purple room wasn't going to make the difference in a sale. But even Isabel's best arguments didn't work. The purple has to go.

4. <u>The Handyman</u>

Before the handyman came, I took the digital camera and photographed my room and everything in it.

Then my parents draped the room in plastic drop cloths. It was like a funeral.

The handyman arrived at 9:00 on Sunday morning. When he left at 7:00 that night, the cracks in the kitchen ceiling had disappeared, the tile in the bathroom was freshly caulked, the porch railing no longer wobbled, and my room was repainted a hideous pale cream color.

My Purple Palace is gone!!!!!!!!!!!

Or mostly gone. Even though he put on two coats of paint on Sunday, he had to come back the next day to put a third and a fourth coat on. My beautiful purple walls kept bleeding through the cream color.

HA!!! They can't get rid of my Purple Palace that easily!!!

Purple RULES!

While the ugly paint dried, I camped on Isabel's floor.

Isabel was SUPER nice to me. She said that my purple room was unique and very special. She said that pale cream was dull, boring, and unimaginative. She wished she could chase away all the purple-hating house hunters.

"What kind of an idiot is scared of a wall color?" she said scornfully.

Then she offered to paint my fingernails and toenails purple.

Now every time I look at my hands or feet, they remind me of my lost purple par-adise—and of my new, improved older sister Isabel.

Thank goodness for Isabel. And for Eva and Alex. At least someone in the Hayes family cares about my feelings!

I'm back in my room again. Even though the bedspread, curtains, and furniture are still purple, it already seems like someone else's room.

Everything is changing so quickly that it's almost like a dream. Or a nightmare.

5. The Open House

On Tuesday, every single real estate agent in the city came through our house. Fortunately, Isabel, Eva, Alex, and I were in school.

The real estate agents were excited about our house. They said they could sell it easily.

Great. We are all totally thrilled.

(Can sarcasm eat through a page? If it can, it will dissolve this page. I wish it would dissolve my parents' decision, instead.)

6. The New House Rules

We have to keep the house ready to be shown by real estate agents at any moment.

Total strangers can walk through our house and look into our closets and bathrooms.

The house has to look like no one actually lives here.

This means that we can't let dishes dry in the drain.

Or put magazines on the table.

And we must never throw dirty towels on the bathroom floor.

When an agent wants to show our house, we have to leave.

We have to find someplace to go for an hour or so. Like the mall, the grocery store, or a friend's house.

This is so people can say whatever they want about our house, like "Isn't that carpet hideous?" Or "What an ugly kitchen" or "The yard is too small."

I hate this! I hate it!! Our house is PERFECT for me, Isabel, Eva, and Alex. No one has the right to criticize it.

Twenty people looked at the house yesterday. Most of them came during the day, while I was in school.

Afterward, Marissa gave us feedback. She said things like, "People love the neighborhood, but they don't like the single bathroom." And "You really need to empty your wastebaskets every single day."

Last night, Isabel, Eva, Alex, and I did our homework in a coffee shop. Our parents bought us all hot chocolate and left us there for an hour. Then they dragged us to the supermarket. When we finally got home, all the lights were off. We had to walk up the front stairs in darkness. Five agents had left their cards in the hallway.

As much as I DON'T want to sell our house, I hope this is over soon.

Chapter 8

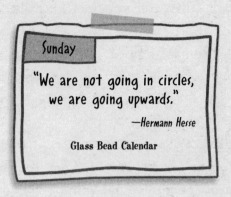

My parents think we're going upward.
They think we're going to sell the house
soon and move to a much better one.

But I say we're going in circles over and
over again.

Downward circles.

We do the same thing every single day.

Every day we pick up the house so it
looks like no one lives here.

Every day we leave the house so that
hordes of strangers can walk through it.

Every day I go to sleep in a sickeningly neat room with cream-colored walls.

I feel like an orphan or an exile from my own home. And we haven't even sold it yet.

Yesterday I spent the day with Hannah. I was glad to get away from real estate agents and obsessive cleaning.

As usual, Hannah had a great idea. She suggested making a friendship collage together. We picked out magazine images that reminded us of things that we did together. We also found some photos of the two of us. And we drew hearts and rainbows and stars in all the empty spaces.

For the first time since our parents made their announcement, I felt happy. At least a little. For a few hours, I almost forgot about the move.

The collage is hanging on Hannah's wall now, but when we move, it'll go to my new room to remind me of my best friend and our friendship.

My new room won't be deep purple like my old one. My parents have told me that I can only paint it a pale purple. It's easier to repaint, if they ever need to. (Why? Are we going to move again?)

Mauve or lilac walls will be better than ugly chalk ones, but I'm still going to hate my new room. And I know I'll hate our new house, too.

Thank goodness I'll have Hannah's and my friendship collage to remind me of everything I love.

"The whole family together!" Olivia said in her new enthusiastic tone of voice. "What a treat this is!"

From the backseat of the Hayes van came grumbling and frowns.

"For whom? I have homework to do," Isabel said in an irritated tone. "This drive is a *total* waste of time."

Alex scowled. He had barely spoken since they got in the car. "I don't want to be here," he said.

Eva tapped her foot impatiently. "You better get me home in time for my practice."

Abby didn't say anything. She continued to stare

glumly out the window at the new developments that were springing up outside the city.

"A happy family outing," Paul commented drily. No one replied.

The Hayes parents were the only cheerful people in the car.

Real estate agents were showing their house this afternoon. Olivia and Paul had decided that they all needed a "lovely Sunday afternoon drive in the country" together.

None of the Hayes kids had wanted to go, but their parents had persuaded, bribed, or ordered them into the van.

As the van exited the garage, Marissa pulled up to the curb. Abby caught a glimpse of the couple looking at the house.

He wore a new leather jacket and his hair was slicked back. She wore lime capris and tottered in very high-heeled sandals.

Abby hated them on sight.

Now she wondered what those people were saying about their house. She hoped that they hated it so they wouldn't buy it, but she didn't want them criticizing anything, either.

In the front seat, her father was humming. Abby

wished he would stop. It was getting on her nerves.

He switched lanes and turned onto an exit ramp, then slowed down before merging into oncoming traffic.

"We're almost there," Paul announced. He headed onto a small private road.

"Where?" Eva demanded.

"Here," their mother answered. "At Misty Acres."

They were pulling into a development so new that huge houses sat on a bare hill. There weren't any lawns yet; the earth was freshly turned over. A tractor sat in front of one of the houses.

"What did we come here for?" Alex asked in a cranky voice.

"To look at new houses," Paul said.

Isabel gasped. *"What?"*

"Didn't you want to be consulted?" her father asked.

"I can't believe you'd even *think* of living in a place like this!" Eva cried.

"I hate it," Alex said simply.

"Let's go home," Abby said with a shudder. The whole place looked barren and empty. There were no people anywhere. It was as different from her old neighborhood as it could possibly be. What were her parents thinking?

"It's under construction," Olivia explained. "This is not how it's going to look in a month. Wait until you see the house."

The van came to a halt.

Olivia was the first to get out. Then Paul stepped out and sniffed the air. "Ah, the country," he said.

Slowly, Abby and her siblings climbed out of the car.

On either side of the brand-new sidewalk, the earth lay in freshly turned clumps with a few stray blades of grass poking through. Trees wrapped in burlap leaned against a shiny new pickup truck.

The houses all looked alike, as if they had been cloned.

"How can anyone tell one house from another?" Abby asked.

Eva elbowed her. "People who live here have a chip implanted in their brains. It beeps when they approach their front door," she said.

"Now, now," their father said. "Don't be so quick to judge."

Alex reached for Isabel's hand. Eva put her arm around Abby's shoulder. Together, the four siblings followed their parents onto the front porch of one of the identical houses.

Abby wondered if all the people who lived here looked alike and thought alike, too. Could a house change your personality?

Abby remembered how her best friend, Jessica, had totally changed after she moved. She had become a different person. Could it happen to *her*, too? Abby hoped not.

Olivia took a key out of her purse and unlocked the door.

The Hayes family stepped into a large entranceway. Skylights flooded the space with light. The floors were a warm, polished wood. There were high ceilings, huge windows everywhere, and polished bannisters. A gleaming staircase led to the second floor.

"Wow," Abby said in spite of herself.

Their mother smiled. "It gets better."

She and Paul led the way through a vast living room, pointing out built-in shelves, window seats, and closets. There was a formal dining room, a library, a family room, and a large, bright kitchen with gleaming new appliances, skylights, and beautiful cherry cupboards.

It was all beautiful, Abby couldn't help thinking,

much more so than their old house. She tried to push away the thought.

Upstairs, the master bedroom had numerous closets, a dressing room, and a private bathroom with a claw-foot tub and skylights.

The kids' bedrooms were twice the size of their old ones. Two had lofts. The closets were room-sized. There were three bathrooms for four bedrooms.

"Isn't this just a tad wasteful?" Isabel asked. "I mean, think of scarce resources like water and electricity."

"If we lived here, we'd use the same amount of water," their mother pointed out. "But no one would have to fight over it."

"So? I like fighting over the bathroom," Abby lied.

She couldn't help wondering what it would be like to never again find that someone had taken her shampoo or used up the last drop of her lotion, to never again discover her towel crumpled on the floor after she had carefully hung it up.

And what would it be like to have a loft as a hideaway, or as a place for sleepovers?

Abby quickly dismissed the disloyal thoughts from

her mind. If her old house had feelings, she didn't want to hurt them.

Her father showed them into the upstairs game room.

"This is totally cool!" Alex cried.

"Not bad," Eva said approvingly. "Do you think someone could get a pool table in here?"

Their father nodded. "A pool table, a couch, and a TV. This is a place for family, friends, and parties."

"You haven't seen it all yet," their mother said. Her eyes were sparkling. "We have to go downstairs again."

Abby groaned. "Do we *have* to?"

"I've seen enough," Isabel said, her nose in the air. "This house isn't for me."

Alex and Eva hurried to agree with them. "We don't like it, either," they said, but without conviction.

Their mother wanted to show off a huge wraparound deck. Their father pointed to an equally huge garage.

"It's big enough to live in," Isabel said sarcastically. "Maybe we could move in there instead."

"There's a studio apartment above the garage,"

Paul said. "I could use it for an office. It even has its own bathroom."

"*Another* bathroom?" Alex cried. "How many do we need? A thousand?"

Their mother pointed to a great hole in the ground. "That's the future swimming pool," she said.

"A swimming pool?" Eva repeated. Her eyes were huge.

"There are tennis courts, too," their mother added. She pointed to a wooded area. "And hiking and cross-country ski trails."

"We might put in a Jacuzzi," Paul said, looking at Isabel.

Isabel shrugged as if she didn't care.

Olivia leaned against the deck railing. "So what do you think of this place, everyone?" she suddenly asked. "Give us your honest opinions."

"It's big," Alex said.

Eva glanced at Isabel and quickly said, "I like it."

"You're *not* serious," Abby said. "I hate it." She waited for Isabel to tell her parents that the house was impossible.

But instead, Isabel looked down at her glossy gold fingernails and mumbled, "It's not bad."

"Not bad?" Abby cried in dismay.

"Admit it, having our own swimming pool, tennis courts, and hiking trails isn't half bad," Eva said.

"The game room is awesome!" Alex added.

"Don't you want your own bathroom?" Isabel said. "Or a library to study in?"

"No," Abby said. "I don't care about any of it." She was furious. How could her siblings betray their old house like this? Someone had to stick up for it, and it looked like it was up to her.

"I hate this house," Abby said again. "It's awful. And I know that *you*"—she looked at her siblings— "will hate it, too. When you come to your senses. Can we see another house now? There's got to be something better out there."

She wasn't sure what she meant by "better." Maybe *"more like the old house."* This house just wasn't the kind of place that the Hayes family lived in. It wasn't the kind of place that *she* lived in.

"I'm afraid not," her father said.

"We put down an offer two days ago," her mother said. "I'm happy that most of you like the house. You will, too, Abby, once you get used to it. We're moving here next month, just in time for my first day at my new job."

Chapter 9

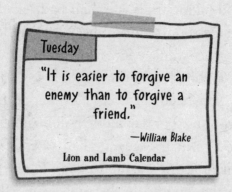

It is easier to forgive an enemy than to forgive a sister. Or a pair of sisters. Or a pair of sisters and a brother. Not to mention my parents!

Who is worse: my parents for making us move, or my siblings for going along with it? I feel let down by everyone.

But I am going to live in Misty Acres, like it or not.

Questions
What kind of a name is Misty Acres?

How can MY family live in a place called Misty Acres?

Do they have fog in their brains?

I'm going to call it Missed Acres.

Because I think my family is really missing something important.

A neighborhood is more important than cherry kitchen cupboards. And friends can't be replaced by a fancy address. Since when has the Hayes family wanted a lot of expensive things, anyway? We've always managed very well without a professional kitchen!

Is there ANYTHING good about this move?

Alex and I are getting loft bedrooms. We are sharing a bathroom. Eva and Isabel each get their own bathroom, but no loft.

We'll also have a swimming pool in our backyard—when it gets finished. Right now, it's a muddy hole.

Someday I can invite all my friends for a pool party. If they can find their way to Missed Acres.

Art class had just begun. Abby frowned in concentration as she tried to capture the brilliant yellow daffodils in a blue vase in front of her.

The other students in Ms. Bean's class were painting bouquets of daffodils, hyacinths, and tulips. The room smelled of spring blossoms.

Across from her, Abby's friend Sophia was studying the daffodils intently. She loved to draw. She was happiest when she had a piece of charcoal or a paintbrush in her hand.

Abby's hand wobbled, and paint streaked across the page. She grabbed a towel to wipe it off.

"I messed up," Abby said to Ms. Bean, who was walking over to her.

"Let it dry and paint over it." There was a smear of blue paint on Ms. Bean's cheek, and her hands were covered with a fine white dust.

"This is hard," Abby complained. "I like collages better. You don't have to worry so much about making mistakes. At least, not the same kind of mistakes."

She glanced toward the front of the room where Ms. Bean had hung her collage on the wall. It cheered her to look at it. Ms. Bean had given her an A+ on the assignment. Thank goodness something had gone right in the past week.

"Have you been making more collages?" her teacher asked.

"Hannah and I made a friendship collage on Saturday," Abby told her. "But I won't be doing any more for a while."

Ms. Bean raised an eyebrow. "Why not?"

"We're moving in a few weeks," Abby said.

"You're not leaving this class, I hope," Ms. Bean said anxiously. "I'd hate to lose you as a student. And you're irreplaceable on *The Daisy* staff."

"I'm leaving the neighborhood, that's all. I'll still be a student at Susan B. Anthony and an editor on *The Daisy*."

"That's good," Ms. Bean began, then stopped when she saw Abby's face. "I guess that's not so good, is it?"

Abby put down her brush. "I don't want to leave my home or my neighborhood."

"I saw the FOR SALE sign in front of your house," Mason said. "I wanted to take it away."

"They'd just put up a new sign," Abby said. "And anyway, someone's about to make an offer on the house. That's what my parents say."

She hoped it wasn't the man in the leather jacket and the woman in the lime capris. If someone *had* to live in their house, she hoped it was a nice young family with babies. Or somebody's grandparents.

"I can't believe you're leaving the neighborhood," Sophia said. "What will I do when you're gone?"

"What will any of us do without Abby?" Mason said.

Listening to them made Abby want to cry.

"The move might not be as bad as you think," Ms. Bean said comfortingly. "You'll still be here with all your friends."

"It's a really bad mistake," Abby said. "Worst of all, my parents bought a fancy house this weekend. I hate it."

"I bet it's not as fancy as *my* house," Brianna interrupted. Today she wore tiny diamonds in her ears. She had on a bright yellow miniskirt, a silk scarf, and a yellow cashmere sweater.

"At my house, we have a swimming pool, a conservatory, and horse stables," Brianna bragged. "The stables are actually a mile away, but still . . ."

"Do you muck out the stables?" Mason asked.

"Of course not!" Brianna sniffed.

"We're going to have a swimming pool, too," Abby said to her. "My parents said I can have a pool party after we move in. Not that I'm going to be in the mood," she added glumly.

"A pool party sounds like fun," Sophia said.

Brianna wasn't impressed. "My house has a small theater," she announced. "I can put on performances for all my friends."

"A captive audience?" Mason suggested.

"Shut up, Mason," Brianna said rudely.

"My new room has a loft," Abby said. Could Brianna's house possibly be fancier than the Hayeses' new house at Missed Acres? It didn't seem possible. "The closet is twice as big as my old bedroom."

"Wow," Sophia breathed.

Brianna dismissed it with a wave of her hand.

"Our new house has a library and a game room, too," Abby continued.

"So?"

"We have tennis courts and hiking trails."

"So do we," Brianna said, not to be bested. "Do you have a Jacuzzi? A carriage house?"

"You mean a four-car garage with an apartment

above it? My father is going to use it for his home office."

"Top *that*, Brianna," Mason crowed.

Abby smiled. She had never once, in her entire life, out-bragged Brianna. It *almost* made the move worthwhile.

"I bet you don't have a hand-polished bannister in the hallway," Brianna shot back. "And skylights."

"We have all of them," Abby said triumphantly. "It sounds like my new house is as good as yours, Brianna. Or better."

"But *we* have the biggest, best house in the entire development," Brianna insisted. "It was designed especially for us. The architect is my father's fifth cousin's niece's husband's brother."

Mason groaned. "Is there anyone you're *not* related to, Brianna?"

"You!" she snapped, tossing back her glossy black hair.

"Like, I'm seriously, so totally, heartbroken," Mason said sarcastically. "This is gonna ruin my day."

Brianna ignored him. "Last week they photographed my house for *Beautiful* magazine," she continued. "It's the most stunning home in Misty Acres."

"*Misty Acres?*" Abby repeated in shock. "Did you say Misty Acres?" She felt as if something had gotten stuck in her throat.

"What's it to you?" Brianna asked.

"My parents just, um, bought a house there," she stammered.

Mason's eyes widened. "They did?"

Abby nodded.

"Which one?" Brianna demanded.

"It has a red door. But they all look alike to me."

Brianna did a pirouette. "*That* house," she said smugly. "It's a sweet little place. But it doesn't measure up to ours."

"Nothing ever does," Mason murmured.

"We'll be neighbors, Abby," Brianna smirked. "My house is at the top of the hill. Like a castle, you know."

"Uh," Abby managed to say.

"I'll give you a tour when you move in," Brianna promised. "It's truly fabulous. You'll see right away that it's absolutely the best."

"Do you ride the school bus?" Abby asked suddenly.

"You'll be able to sit with *me*," Brianna promised. "I bet you're looking forward to that!"

"Can't wait," Abby mumbled. Now, in addition to everything else, she'd be forced to listen to nonstop bragging twice a day. Would she be able to stand it?

Or would she be so lonely for friends in faraway Misty Acres that she'd feel grateful even for Brianna's boasting?

Chapter 10

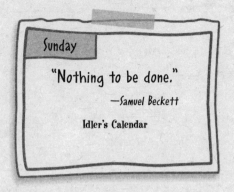

Sunday

"Nothing to be done."

—Samuel Beckett

Idler's Calendar

There is nothing to be done about:

1. The move to Missed Acres.

2. Leaving the neighborhood.

3. My beloved purple room painted over.

4. The offer made on our house.

5. The fact that we're moving very soon.

6. The fact that my siblings act as if it's okay.

7. The fact that Brianna will be our new neighbor!

On the other hand, there is EVERY-
THING to be done!

1. Dad is getting rid of tires and junk in
the basement.

2. Mom is cleaning out the attic.

3. Alex, Isabel, Eva, and I are sorting
through our possessions.

4. All trash goes to the dump.

5. Anything usable goes to charity.

6. After that, we have to pack whatever's left.

7. We have to place
every single book in a box.

8. We have to wrap every
dish and glass in newspaper
or bubble wrap.

9. We have to put towels and
bedding in duffel bags.

10. We have to label all cartons, boxes,
and bags and color code everything, too.

I wish that this was reversed.

I wish I could do EVERYTHING to stop
this move, and I wish there was NOTHING
I had to do to make it happen.

This is the hardest work I've done in my life. The more we do, the more there's left to do.

Everyone is cracking under the strain.

The Haywire Hayes Household

Mom
Has cobwebs in her hair and streaks of dirt on her face. Crawls on hands and knees into filthy corners of the attic to retrieve ancient objects that no one has seen for hundreds of years.

Hands objects to Dad, who stares at them for a few minutes, then throws them in trash bag.

Dad
When not throwing things in trash is on the phone, arguing with movers.

Isabel
Very busy hand-wrapping approximately two billion tiny bottles of nail polish in cotton wool.

Eva

Throws her clothes in garbage bags. Puts muddy sports equipment and filthy cleats in suitcases.

For unknown reason, sleeps on floor in sleeping bag. (Preparing self for harsh conditions in new, luxurious home?)

Alex

Barricades bedroom door. Mutters darkly that "no one better touch my robots, or else."

Obsessively sorts and labels every tiny little block or electronic part he owns.

Me

Packing up an entire life-time of journals and sealing them into box with MILES of duct tape. (Am calling it the Journal Fortress.) Am not sure if I'll ever be able to open it again.

Have packed fifteen boxes of calendars so far. (No comment.)

* * *

We are all very tired and getting more and more cranky. This is like a war, except that there aren't any dead bodies (yet).

My traitorous sisters, Eva and Isabel, are trying to help me "accept" the move.

Isabel says that the move is a "done deal," and that I can either "choose to be happy" or "choose to be miserable."
Her argument stinks.
If I can choose my happiness, then I choose THIS house and THIS neighborhood.

I think Isabel chooses to make our parents happy instead of us. Why did she make that choice? Did they bribe her with a lifetime supply of nail polish?

Eva says that Missed Acres is an amazing place and that I'll grow to love it. She rants about the loft bedrooms, swimming pool, four-car garage, and many bathrooms.

HUH?????

I'm supposed to get excited about a garage and some bathrooms?

My older sisters can't change my feelings. I'll NEVER accept the move. <u>This</u> is my home. This is where my friends are. This is where I belong.

To make things even worse, we have a buyer for our house.

It's Mr. Leather Jacket and Mrs. Lime Capris. They came to the house again this weekend, bringing their three little children with them.

This time, we didn't have to leave our house when they toured it.

This time, I wish we had.

When the family came into my room, I was packing up my books.

They stared at my purple furniture, purple

bedspread, and purple curtains.

"I hate purple," the oldest kid, a boy with a mullet, declared.

"Me, too," said a littler one. She wore shiny pink ballerina shoes and a frilly pink dress with lots of bows. She looked like a Brianna-in-training.

The littlest boy didn't talk. He buried his head in his mother's shoulder and sucked his thumb.

Their mother said soothingly, "It's not a very nice color, is it? But don't worry, we won't have any purple in _our_ house. Maybe we'll paint this room pink."

The father said, "But first, I'm going to take down this wall, kids, and open everything up. Right now it's kind of cramped in here, but it'll be a whole different room by the time we get through with it."

I tried to glare at them, but they didn't notice. Maybe they thought I was another old part of the room on its way out.

When I told my parents about this conversation, they just shrugged. My parents didn't react even when I told them that they were going to paint my room pink!! Pink!!! My least favorite color in the universe!!

I bet it won't be a lovely rose color, either. It'll probably be plastic pink, or diarrhea-medicine pink.

Whenever I complained, my parents only replied that Mr. Leather Jacket and Mrs. Lime Capris had made a very decent offer on the house.

In a month or two, Mr. Leather Jacket and Mrs. Lime Capris will have the mortgage, the title search, the insurance, and all the other boring stuff they need before signing the papers.

Then our house will be theirs, to do with as they want. They can punch holes in the walls, paint the entire house the color of bubble gum, or turn the garden into a parking lot.

And just like Isabel says, there's nothing I can do about it.

Chapter 11

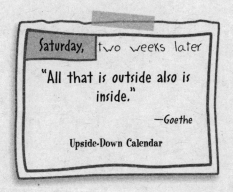

Saturday, two weeks later

"All that is outside also is inside."

—Goethe

Upside-Down Calendar

All of our furniture, clothes, books, dishes, and pots are outside our house. They are also inside the moving van.

In a few hours, all the stuff that is outside will be inside our new house at Missed Acres.

Yes, we're moving today.

I'm writing in tiny letters so my journal will know how depressed I feel about the move.

My journal has probably figured that out

already, because I haven't written in it for two weeks.

Usually I never stop writing, no matter what. But this time, I couldn't write at all.

This is my last journal entry in the old house. I'm sitting on the empty floor of my empty, formerly purple room. There's nothing left here, except the dents in the floor. And me.

It's so strange being inside with everything outside. I feel like a ghost in my own house.

Maybe I'll come back to haunt the Leather Jacket and Lime Capris family. Ha! It'll serve them right for painting my room pink.

Note: They haven't painted it yet. They can't touch my room until they buy the house. That won't happen for at least another six weeks. We still own it!

Even if we don't live here anymore, the house is still ours.

For me, this will ALWAYS be our house, no matter what. This will always be my true home.

Surrounded by boxes of all sizes in her new room in Misty Acres, Abby looked for the next one to unpack.

A few hours ago, the movers had brought everything into the new house. They had deposited all the boxes in their proper rooms, brought in the furniture, checked to make sure nothing was left in the truck, and then left.

The Hayes family was now officially moved in. Well, sort of.

The house was in total chaos. Abby's room was no exception.

Going over to one of the cartons, Abby slit open the top and reached in. Her hand closed around her stapler. She brought it over to the new rolltop desk.

Her mother had insisted on replacing her old furniture. She had told Abby that a painted purple desk and bureau wouldn't fit in the Misty Acres bedroom. They were the wrong color, the wrong size, and the wrong shape. Only a new desk, bureau, and bed would do.

No matter how hard Abby argued, her mother wouldn't be swayed.

Abby had cried when they took away the old furniture. Eva and Isabel, on the other hand, had cheered when the truck came to pick up *their* old things.

Now she kneeled down to scoop up an armful of books. She quickly scanned the titles. Most were volumes from her favorite series. She knew exactly where she wanted to put them—upstairs in the loft.

Abby had to climb a sturdy wooden ladder to get there. Her mother had furnished the loft with a new purple futon, a reading lamp, and a bookshelf. It was warm, cozy, and welcoming. Abby had to admit it was pretty nice. It was like her own private tree house.

Earlier, she'd brought up her journal, a supply of pens, and the friendship collage to hang on the wall. Now she arranged the books on a shelf and sat down on the futon for a moment.

With a sigh, she got up again and went down to the room of boxes. It was going to take days to unpack. Or maybe even weeks.

Someone knocked on the door.

"Come in!" Abby yelled. "If you dare!"

Eva surveyed the mess. "Looks better than my room," she said.

"Really?" Abby said in disbelief.

"I haven't even started to unpack my stuff." Her sister collapsed on Abby's new double bed. "I've been helping Mom look for the pots and pans. We can't find them anywhere. Are they here?"

"*Here?* No way."

"This is a nightmare," Eva pronounced.

Isabel came into the room. "There's no water in my bathroom," she said. "I can't wash my hair."

"So? You washed it yesterday. What's the big deal?" her twin asked.

"Never mind," Isabel said crossly. "I just have to."

"Is it that cute guy who lives two houses down?" Eva demanded. "*I* saw him first."

"So? You don't own him!" Isabel shot back.

"Hey, no fighting in my room," Abby commanded.

Before any one of them could say another word, their mother appeared.

"I called the movers," she announced. "*They* don't know where the pots are, either."

"Pots?" Isabel repeated. "There's no water in my bathroom."

"We won't be able to cook if we don't find them," Olivia said.

Alex poked his head in the door. "I have a headache," he said. "And it smells like chemicals everywhere."

"It's probably the new carpet." Olivia rubbed her neck.

"You have to open all the windows," Isabel said to Alex. "Don't shut them until the chemical smell disappears."

Eva put her arm around Alex's shoulder. "Want to sleep on the deck tonight?"

"In a tent?" Alex said eagerly. "Yes!!!"

"Good luck finding one," Abby muttered.

It was impossible to find almost anything, except by accident. Her mother had insisted on labeling boxes, but then you had to find the boxes. That was hard when they were stacked floor to ceiling in every room.

"Is anyone hungry? Or are we all too busy unpacking to think of food?" Olivia pulled her cell phone from a pocket. "It's way past lunchtime. Anyone up for ordering a pizza?"

They all started talking at once.

"Order barbecued-chicken pizza," Isabel said.

"Pepperoni!" Eva cried.

"Plain cheese," Alex said.

"I like artichoke pizza," Abby said.

Their mother sighed. "Can you narrow it down a bit? To maybe two or three toppings?"

Just as a fresh round of arguments broke out, Paul Hayes appeared. He was wearing a ripped sweatshirt and old jeans. There was dark stubble on his chin. He looked exhausted.

"Bad news," he announced.

"Aside from the missing pots?" Eva asked.

"Aside from the chemical smell?" Alex asked.

"Aside from my dirty hair?" Isabel said.

"You want a different pizza topping from everyone else," his wife joked.

"I wish," their father said wearily.

Abby shrugged. As far as she was concerned, the *move* was bad news. What could be worse than what had already happened?

Their father ran a filthy hand through his hair. "It's the water pump. I think there's something seriously wrong with it."

"You mean . . . ?" Eva said.

He nodded. "No water in the house."

Isabel turned pale.

"Oh, no," Olivia said softly. She looked like she wanted to be on another planet.

"I can't believe it." Alex cried. "We have a brand-new house and no water!"

Abby had to swallow the words that leaped into her mind: *I knew this was a bad idea.*

Chapter 12

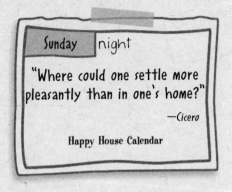

Sunday night

"Where could one settle more pleasantly than in one's home?"

—Cicero

Happy House Calendar

It's not very pleasant in this house.

1. We have no water.

We have to wait until Dad can reach the people who installed the pump. They are not at their office over the weekend.

Dad went to the supermarket and bought dozens of jugs of water so that we have enough to drink, to make tea, to wash our hands, etc.

BUT . . .

We can't take baths or showers in our new bathrooms.

We can't do the laundry in our new machines.

We can't wash the dishes in our new dishwasher.

We're not supposed to flush any of our four toilets more than once a day. UGH!

Note to the Hayes parents (not that they'll listen): In our old house, we had only one toilet, but we could flush it as much as we wanted.

We're desperate!!!

Some of us have sneaked out to use the portable toilets that the construction crew left. (I hope Brianna doesn't see us.)

2. We can't cook.

The pots are still missing! Plus, we don't have water. Duh.

We warm things up in the microwave. Popcorn, anyone?

We're also eating frozen pizza, frozen waffles, yogurt, and protein bars. Oh, yeah, and jar food, like peanut butter and jelly.

Okay, we're not starving, but the food is seriously disgusting.

3. The carpets have a chemical smell that's giving everyone, not just Alex, headaches.

Eva, Isabel, and Alex dragged mattresses out on the deck last night.

Dad and Mom slept in the garage.

I slept on the floor underneath my wide-open windows.

Not one single person in the Hayes family is getting a good night's sleep.

4. Everyone is in a bad, I mean _bad_, mood.

Of course we are.

We don't have bathrooms, running water, showers, decent food, or a comfortable place to sleep. And we're being poisoned by toxic fumes.

Plus, we're confused. We were supposed to move into a spacious, new, luxurious dream-house.

But it seems more like a nightmare camping trip!

I called Hannah this afternoon to tell her about all the disasters. (Thank goodness the telephones work.)

She invited me to spend the night at her house and walk to school tomorrow morning with her and Mason.

But my parents said no. They said that we were too busy unpacking. They said that it would take an hour from their day to drive back and forth to Hannah's house. They said that now that we live in Misty Acres, I have to give them more advance notice when I want a ride.

So . . . no overnight at Hannah's. No shower, no toilet, no comfortable bed, no good food, and, worst of all, no best friends to walk to school with tomorrow morning.

Chapter 13

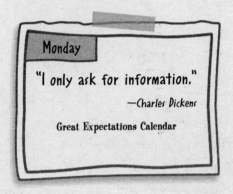

Monday

"I only ask for information."

—Charles Dickens

Great Expectations Calendar

<u>Information I Have TRIED to Ask For</u>

1. When will we have water?

2. When I come home from school today, will everyone still be in a bad mood?

3. How many nights will we have to sleep in strange, uncomfortable places?

4. When will we be allowed to flush our toilets?

5. Will the pots show up?

6. How many billions of boxes are left to be unpacked?

7. Will "normal" life ever start happening again?

Information I Have Received

NONE.

I mean zero, zip, zilch.

Even when I <u>beg</u> for information, I don't get it.

Mom and Dad shake their heads and say infuriating things like "I wish I knew" or "Your guess is as good as mine" or "Be patient, Abby, this will work out sooner or later."

That's easy for them to say. Dad works in a home office. Mom has taken the week off.

But Isabel, Eva, Alex, and I have to go to school this morning.

We're kind of dirty.

We've all been eating strange food combinations.

We've been sleeping on floors and decks.

Most of our clothes are still in boxes.

We are malnourished, sleep deprived, badly dressed, and not very clean.

AND we have to go on the school bus for the first time this morning! We have to face new kids, a long bus ride, and on top of everything else, <u>Brianna</u>!!!

"And then they installed a hand-cut crystal chandelier in our dining hall," Brianna said. "It casts rainbow lights on the French hand-knotted tapestry and the hand-polished marble fireplace."

"Uh, very nice." Abby yawned, wondering if Brianna ever got tired of boasting.

Did she participate in some sort of braggers' strength-training program? Did she boast to her own reflection in the bathroom mirror every morning to keep in shape?

Abby couldn't help smiling at the thought.

"And I have the *whitest* teeth," she imagined Brianna saying. "My toothbrush is made of hand-tooled bristles."

If only Hannah or Natalie or Mason were here to share the joke with! But they were walking home from school without her.

Abby was far away from her friends, trapped next to Brianna.

At least it was the end of the day. Brianna hadn't been on the school bus that morning. She had a doctor's appointment and had been driven to school.

"How is your sweet little house?" Brianna asked.

"Fine," Abby lied. She wished she hadn't washed in a bowl of cold water before getting dressed this morning. If she had smelled really bad, Brianna might not have sat next to her.

If they were going to ride the bus together every day, she'd have to buy a Brianna repellent.

Was there a product called Brag-away, Boast-X, or Best Begone at the local camping store? Or a Boast Buster?

If they didn't have one, she'd invent it. She'd call it a besticide.

It was another funny thought she couldn't share with her friends.

"I bet you're just *dying* to see my house," Brianna continued.

The bus pulled into the Misty Acres development and came to a stop. Abby glanced at the top of the hill where Brianna's house reigned supreme. Funny. From down here, it looked exactly like hers.

Abby stood up. "Sorry, I have to unpack," she said.

Brianna picked up her white leather backpack. "I know what it's like to move," she said dramatically. "We had no mirrors for five whole days!"

"How tragic for you," Abby murmured.

"I'm a survivor," Brianna said.

The bus doors opened. Abby followed Brianna out of the crowded school bus. Was this her future?

On the brand-new sidewalk, Brianna waved good-bye to Abby. "See you tomorrow!"

I can't wait, Abby thought. She slowly turned toward her new house. She wondered what was waiting for her there.

"I'm home!" Abby yelled a few minutes later. It felt wrong to say the word "home." This wasn't her home; it would never be. She ought to use another word, but she couldn't think of one. Or maybe she ought to speak in another language.

Her words echoed around the hallway as if they didn't know where to go, either. No one answered. Had the house swallowed up her family?

Not that she expected to find her siblings at home— they always had someplace better to be. Abby walked into the living room. The boxes had disappeared. The couches faced each other; unfamiliar lamps stood on side tables, and paintings hung on the walls. It was like someone else's house. She stood there for a moment, then made her way to the kitchen.

Olivia Hayes was unpacking dishes with a group of women. She was smiling and talking as she worked.

"Um, hi, Mom," Abby said awkwardly. She didn't know most of the women who were putting away the Hayes family plates, glasses, and silverware. Where had they come from?

"This is my daughter Abby," Olivia announced.

Abby raised a hand in greeting.

"These new friends came to help us," Olivia gushed. "They're members of the Misty Acres Jogging Club. I met them this morning. Aren't they wonderful? I can't believe how much they've done."

New friends? Had her mother gotten a new life along with the new house?

"Your house is gorgeous, Abby," one woman said.

"So is your room," another added.

Abby stared at her. Had her mother showed them her room? Her messy room, full of boxes?

As if she could read her daughter's mind, Olivia said, "Your room is cleaner than you think."

No, it isn't, Abby thought.

"We brought cookies," one of the friends was saying, pointing to a tray of home-baked cookies. "Help yourself."

"Thanks," Abby mumbled. "Thanks for helping us."

"Do you have homework?" her mother asked.

"Not much. I did it in study hall." Abby cleared her throat. She *had* to ask. "Uh, Mom. Do we have . . . um, *water*?"

With a dramatic flourish, Olivia Hayes went over to the sink and turned on the tap. Water gushed out. "Behold, the water!"

"Mom?" Abby said. Her mother was acting giddy. Was it the friends? Or the move?

"They came today and fixed everything," Olivia said.

"You mean, I can take a shower?" Abby said.

Her mother unwrapped an ice-cream glass from its cocoon of newspaper. "You don't need permission from me."

Laughter followed her out of the kitchen. Abby slowly climbed the stairs to her room.

Some people had all the luck, she thought resentfully. Her mother's new friends had come over to help. But *Abby's* friends couldn't just hop in their cars or on their bikes. They had to ask for rides, then wait for their parents to say yes.

If Abby needed help unpacking or just wanted a friendly face to keep her company, she'd have to plan days or even weeks in advance.

Unless, like her mother, she made new friends in Misty Acres. She hoped there was someone besides Brianna. She hadn't seen anyone else her age waiting for the school bus this morning.

But even if she made dozens of new friends, today she'd have to face her room alone.

As she opened her bedroom door, Abby braced herself for the mess that awaited her. But the boxes and suitcases were gone.

Abby blinked as if she couldn't quite believe it. She walked into the room and looked around in wonder.

What happened while she was in school today? Had some fairy godmother waved her wand over everything?

Her books were on the shelves; the newest calendars hung on the walls. Someone had hung a picture above her desk.

She stared in shock. Wasn't *she* supposed to have done this?

Her double bed, under the loft, had a new purple quilt. Purple pillows were plumped up by the headboard. There was a pale purple gauzy curtain that surrounded the bed like a canopy.

Abby ran to the closet. Her clothes hung neatly on the rods; her games lay organized on the shelves. Her shoes were lined up on one wall; her sports equipment was neatly arranged.

"Mom!" she said, shaking her head. It had to be her mother. How had she found time to do it?

Now that the room was set up, Abby could really see it.

She had a reading and writing loft. She had a canopy bed with a purple veil. She even had a table that she could use for collages.

It wasn't bad. It was even quite nice. She had to admit that she couldn't have improved on it.

The room had everything she needed. But it wasn't quite *hers*. Abby still felt as if she didn't belong here.

Chapter 14

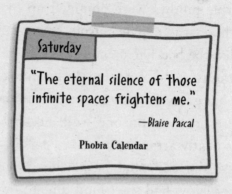

Saturday

"The eternal silence of those infinite spaces frightens me."

—Blaise Pascal

Phobia Calendar

I know just what he means.

What he says describes this house perfectly. It's WAY too big and quiet.

We have now lived here for a week.
It looks like a home, but it's still not OUR home.
OUR home was cozy and warm.
In OUR home, you never missed anyone. Everyone was always bumping into one another, fighting over bathroom time, or barging into each others' rooms.

Okay, I admit that I hated the fighting. And we do have fewer fights here. But that's only because you can never find anyone to fight with!

The new house is vast and silent. It's a place that you can get lost in. It's a place where you can spend hours looking for a family member. People disappear in this house.

<u>What We Need in Our New, Huge House</u>
1. Maps of all the rooms, closets, hallways, and bathrooms.
2. Pagers for everyone.
3. Closed-circuit television?
4. Tracking skills.
5. A smaller house inside the bigger one?

Today I made a collage from photos of our old house.

It was our old house, but somehow I couldn't remember what it felt like to live there. It made me feel very sad. I had planned to hang the collage next to the friendship collage I made with Hannah, but I hid it in a drawer instead.

What Else I Did During My First Saturday in Our New House

1. Talked to Hannah for a long time on the phone.
2. Talked to Sophia.
3. Talked to Mason.
4. Wished that all of them were at my house.
5. Spent a long time searching for parents to ask if I could invite friends over.
6. Found parents, who said "not today."
7. Played game by self in new, luxurious game room.
8. Watched cartoon by self in new, luxurious game room.
9. Took walk by self in new, luxurious housing development.
10. Bumped into Brianna.
11. Made excuses for not visiting her new, luxurious house that is supposedly better than ours.

12. Went back to our new, luxurious house.

13. Took long shower in new, luxurious bathroom.

14. Had dinner with family in new, formal dining room.

15. Parents left to see movie.

16. Siblings disappeared into new, luxurious rooms.

17. Called Hannah again.

18. Called Sophia again.

19. Called Mason again.

20. Flipped through address book, looking for friends to call.

21. Called Natalie.

22. Called Bethany.

23. Called Casey.

24. Almost called Brianna, but stopped self in time.

It's bedtime. Thank goodness! I can't wait for this day to be over.

Abby lay awake in the dark. Unable to sleep, she tossed and turned. She reached for the radio and turned on the music. It seemed to come from a faraway place. She switched it off. She knew her sisters and brother were also in their rooms, but the house seemed deserted. Did they mind? Did they even notice?

Her parents hadn't returned from the movies yet. She listened for their van in the driveway. All she heard was the wind in the trees.

A knock sounded at her door.

"Come in!" she called.

"It's me," Isabel said. She was barefoot and wearing fleece pajamas. Her hair was braided around her head. "I can't sleep."

"Me, neither," Abby said.

Isabel sat down on the bed next to Abby. For a few minutes, neither of them said anything.

Then Isabel said, "Remember how we used to snuggle all the time?"

"You mean when I was little?"

"Eva and I would fight over you."

"Did you think I was a toy?"

"You were *so* cute with your curly red hair," Isabel said. "And you imitated whatever Eva and I did."

"Really?"

"Eva taught you to say things like 'Isabel is stupid,' and then I'd teach you to say 'Eva is an idiot.'"

Abby rolled her eyes. "No wonder I'm so messed up."

"You are *not*," Isabel said.

"Oh, yeah?" Abby retorted. "Now I know who to blame."

"Very funny," Isabel said. She stretched out next to Abby. "Who do *I* get to blame?"

"Mom and Dad?"

Isabel didn't answer. "This house scares me sometimes," she said instead.

"It's too big," Abby agreed.

"It's too strange and new."

"I hate it."

"Everything?"

"Um, well, not everything," Abby admitted. "I guess if this house was in our old neighborhood, I'd like it better. I might even love it."

"That's the problem," Isabel said. "The neighborhood."

"Didn't I tell you?" Abby couldn't resist saying. "I knew this was a bad idea."

Isabel didn't say anything, but she sighed deeply.

Abby cupped her hands behind her head and stretched out. "Do you realize that I'm going to have to spend the rest of my life avoiding Brianna?"

"I truly, deeply, sincerely sympathize," Isabel said.

There was another knock at the door.

"Come in!" Abby called again.

Eva tiptoed into the room. She was wearing bunny pajamas. There was medicated cream on her face.

"I'm not waking you up, Abby?" she whispered. Then she saw Isabel. "What are you doing here?"

"What are *you* doing here?"

"Move over," Eva ordered Isabel. "Make room for me."

"Do I have to?" Isabel said, but she made space for her twin.

"This is so cozy," Eva said.

"It was until you showed up," Isabel retorted.

"No fighting in my room," Abby said, then added, "unless you're fighting over me."

Isabel nudged Eva. "Remember how we used to play with Abby when she was a baby?"

Eva grinned. "We used to teach her bad words."

"Serious?" Abby said.

"You repeated them for hours. Mom wasn't happy."

"We pretended that we didn't know where you learned them," Eva added.

"I think Mom knew," Isabel said.

Abby threw a pillow at her sisters. "I was an innocent little baby!"

"Innocent?" Eva repeated. "You'd steal my favorite toys and chew on them."

"And you'd rip pages out of my books," Isabel said.

Abby groaned.

"You were adorable," Eva said fondly.

"*Sometimes,*" Isabel teased. She squeezed Abby's hand. "It's great, all of us together like this. Isn't it? I've missed you, Abby, even though you've been right here!"

The door opened again.

"Abby?" Alex said, "I can't sleep."

Abby, Eva, and Isabel started to laugh.

"Are you having a party?" their little brother asked in a plaintive voice. "Can I join?"

Abby edged closer to the wall. "I think there's room for one more person here."

Alex climbed in next to Eva. Now everyone was crushed together.

"Ouch!" Eva cried. "Stop squirming! You have sharp elbows, Alex." She edged toward Isabel.

"Have you clipped your toenails in the last year, Eva?" Isabel accused her.

"Your braid is tickling my nose," Eva complained.

"I can't move," Abby said, trying to shift her position. She was pinned against the wall. "It's *way* too crowded in here. Can everyone move just an inch?"

Everyone nudged, wiggled, and pushed. The gentle pushes became not so gentle. The bed erupted in wails, shouts, and shoves.

Suddenly, the overhead light flooded on. "What on *earth* is going on in here?" Olivia Hayes demanded.

Everyone froze.

"Mom?" Abby said. "You're back from the movie?"

"You're making enough noise for twenty people," their mother said. "Why aren't you in your own rooms?"

The four Hayes siblings looked guiltily at one another.

"We're, uh, keeping each other company," Eva finally said.

"It sounded like you were killing each other."

"Not really," Isabel said. "I mean, we were only killing each other for a minute or two."

Abby tried to explain. "Nobody could sleep."

Their mother wasn't impressed. "Abby and Alex,

it's way past your bedtime. Eva and Isabel, I left you in charge."

"Sorry, Mom," the twins said.

"It's not their fault!" Abby sprang to her sisters' defense. "This house is too big. We *needed* to be together."

"It just kind of happened," Eva said.

"Like spontaneous combustion," Isabel added.

Their mother didn't reply. "Alex?" she said.

He stumbled to his feet and took her hand. Together they left the room.

For a moment, no one said anything.

"Well, I guess that's the end of that," Eva finally said. She got up and brushed off her bunny pajamas. "Good night, Abby. Good night, Isabel." She disappeared into the hallway.

Isabel sat up cross-legged in the bed. "Do you have enough room to breathe now?"

"I think so," Abby said, stretched out under the covers.

"I'm finally getting sleepy." Isabel leaned over and planted a kiss on her forehead. "Good night, then."

"Good night!" Abby called. Isabel tiptoed out of the room, turned off the light, and closed Abby's door.

With a sigh, Abby leaned back on the pillow. Somehow the house didn't seem quite as strange or big now. Somehow she felt a little more optimistic. She closed her eyes and huddled deeper under the covers.